398
Cha

5052 A

TALES from
OLD CHINA

A collection of Chinese folk tales, fairy tales, and fables

TALES from OLD CHINA

by Isabelle C. Chang

illustrated by Tony Chen

 Random House · New York

For Pancho, Claudia and Pamela
...an echo of your heritage

Contents

Fables from the Far East

The Fox and the Fish

A fox saw a fish darting back and forth near the middle of a river. He asked, "Friend Fish, why don't you swim one way or the other?"

The fish replied, "If I go one way, I shall be swept over the waterfall and perish; if I swim the opposite way, a fisherman with a net hopes to catch me."

"Ah, my friend," said the cunning fox, "why not come ashore and avoid both dangers?"

"No, thank you," answered the fish. "My mother warned me that it is always safer to put up with known dangers than to face un- known ones."

🀄 *Do not jump from the frying pan into the fire.*

The Clockmaker and the Timekeeper

There was once a clockmaker who had a shop in the center of the village. Every day a man stopped by and looked in the window, before hurrying on his way. After a year, the clockmaker hailed the man one day and asked him why he always hesitated by the window, but never entered the shop.

The man replied, "I am the timekeeper for the town, and I have to ring the church bells at exactly twelve o'clock noon. To be accurate, I always check with your clock first."

"Ah," said the clockmaker, "but I always set my clock after I hear the chimes of the church bells."

🀄 *The world is made up of the blind leading the blind.*

Unanswerable Questions

Three merchants arrived at the kingdom of the Dragon Emperor. Each asked the Emperor a question. The ruler summoned all his wise men but none knew the answers.

"Why not ask your fool?" suggested the Empress.

"Where is my fool?" shouted the Emperor.

"He went for a ride on his donkey because you were busy," replied an aide, "but I will go and fetch him right away."

In a short time the fool came in, riding astride his donkey. He dismounted and knelt before the Emperor, murmuring, "What do you desire, Your Majesty?"

"Each of our guests has a question. Answer each one!" commanded the Emperor.

The first merchant asked, "Where is the earth's navel?"

"On the ground, directly below my donkey's belly button," replied the fool.

"How can one be that certain?" asked the astonished merchant.

"If you will not take my word for it, go and measure it yourself. If you find that I am the slightest bit off, come and discuss it with me again," invited the fool.

This left the first merchant with nothing else to say, so the second merchant stepped forth and asked, "What is the exact number of stars in the heavens?"

"The same number as the grains of sand on which my donkey stepped," came the fool's quick reply.

"Prove that," said the second merchant.

"You start counting and if you are still dissatisfied come and see me again."

This left the second merchant speechless, so the third merchant stepped forward and said, "Tell me the number of hairs I have in my beard."

"Your beard has the same number of hairs as is on the back of my donkey."

"How is it possible to count the hairs on your donkey's back?" asked the indignant merchant.

"This is precisely the problem. How is it possible to answer any of the questions you three raise?"

🀫 *Ask a foolish question, get a foolish answer.*

God of the Kitchen

Aeons ago there lived an old gentleman named Chang Kung. Within his compound four generations of his huge family lived in peaceful harmony. Even the numerous dogs of the family did not fight.

This unusually fine family became famous throughout the kingdom. In time the Emperor of the Dragon Throne heard of the Changs, and on one of his annual pilgrimages to the Eastern Mountain, the Emperor stopped to pay them a visit.

In a long solemn procession, the Emperor and members of his court marched up to the Chang gates. Gentle Chang Kung greeted his Emperor on bended knees with bowed head.

"Old One," began the Emperor, "it is said only peace reigns within your gates."

"Your Royal Highness," answered Chang Kung, "it is not for your humble servant to say. Please give great honor to this simple household by seeing for yourself, O Most High."

The Emperor and his men went from court

to court. They questioned and observed each person from the head of the family down to the youngest toddler. Kindness reigned throughout the clan.

Before the Emperor departed he wanted Chang Kung's secret for keeping harmony among so many people.

Old Chang ordered his servants to bring his ink stick and brush. In his best calligraphy, he wrote one hundred characters on a bamboo tablet. With both hands he presented the tablet to his emperor.

"What is this?" asked the bewildered Emperor. "You wrote the same word one hundred times."

"Yes, Most High," replied old Chang, "that word 'Love' contains the only secret to peace."

The Emperor was so impressed that he sang high praises of Chang Kung, whose fame thus grew greater than ever. From every corner of the kingdom people begged for paintings of Chang Kung. They placed his picture over the family hearth. In their hearts they prayed they might grow to love as deeply as he so that harmony might reign in their homes, which in turn would bring order to their country and ultimately peace to the world. That was how the saintly Chang became the famous Kitchen God.

🀫 *If there is right in the soul,*
There will be beauty in the person;
If there is beauty in the person,
There will be love in the home;
If there is love in the home,
There will be order in the nation;
If there is order in the nation,
There will be peace in the world.

The World's Work

An elephant saw a hummingbird lying on its back with its feet in the air.

"What is the matter with you?" asked the elephant.

"I heard that the sky is going to fall today," replied the bird.

"Hrrumph!" snorted the elephant. "Do you think your feeble feet could uphold the heavens?"

"Everyone has to do what he can," retorted the hummingbird.

🀫 *From each according to his ability.*

Ma Ki

Once upon a time there lived a poor family consisting of a farmer, his wife, and son. No matter how hard they tried, they were never able to free themselves from debt to the landlord. Each year their debt grew larger and larger. At last there was nothing they could call their own.

After they had pawned all their extra clothing, it did not seem there was anything more they could lose. But one day they were surprised to see the landlord approaching as they were sitting down for supper. When they were unable to produce the rent upon demand, the landlord snatched away their pot of rice. That night they had to go to bed hungry. Thereafter they often went to bed on empty stomachs.

In time the old farmer died from years of starvation. His wife raised the boy, Ma Ki, as well as she could. These two continued to seek out a living tilling the land, until one day her heart gave out and she fell over her hoe.

Ma Ki buried his mother. Bitterly, he blamed the landlord for all the trouble they had suffered. "Never again," he vowed, "will I hand over another ear of corn to the landlord."

With that thought in mind, he divided the corn into two piles. Then he traded one pile to a hunter for two foxes, and the other for two dozen hens.

He kept one fox hidden in the cellar of his house. Around the other, he tied a rope so he could exercise him daily.

Then one morning Ma Ki met the landlord on one of his rent-collecting rounds.

Seeing Ma Ki with a fox, the landlord exclaimed, "Why, man, what are you doing walking around with a fox? Don't you know it will get away?"

"Not this one," said Ma Ki smiling. He bent down to stroke the fox lovingly, and murmured, "Go, my precious, and bring back some fat chickens." As soon as he untied the fox, the animal bounded off in a flash. Then Ma Ki stood up and said, "Will you do me the honor of coming to my house for chicken dinner tomorrow?"

The landlord was speechless, so he just nodded.

Dinner was ready at high noon. Oh, what a chicken feast was spread on the table! There was a dish of crisp chicken skin to whet the appetite; there was red stewed chicken coddled in wine; there were cold chicken slices; there was a whole steamed chicken that contained soup inside itself; and there was a barbecued chicken done to a golden brown. The aroma from this mixture made the landlord's mouth water before he even entered the house.

Ma Ki and the landlord sat down to dinner without further ceremony. The landlord gorged himself with the delicious chicken dishes. After he had eaten all he could hold, he began to wish he had such a valuable fox. He said, "Ma Ki, let's have a look at your fox."

Ma Ki brought out the other fox he had kept hidden.

"Mm . . . . not a bad fox," mused the landlord. "Will you sell it for a hundred pieces of silver?"

"No, no!" said Ma Ki. "I need never starve as long as I have this fox. You can have your rent money, but I can't part with the fox."

"Ma Ki, you need never pay me any more rent if you sell me that fox for two hundred pieces of silver."

Ma Ki sighed, "Who am I to deny you anything? If you want the fox that much you may have him, but I cannot let him go for less than three hundred pieces of silver plus free rent."

"You drive a hard bargain," said the landlord, but he seemed glad to pay the money and take the fox home.

. 14 . When he returned to his house, he ran boasting to his family about this wonderful fox that had been trained to steal chickens. His wife sneered at his boastfulness.

To prove his point, he bent down and stroked the fox, saying, "Go, my precious, and bring back some fat chickens." As soon as he untied the fox it leaped off and ran into the woods.

The landlord waited for a week and the fox never returned. He finally realized that he had been duped. "The scoundrel! How dare that Ma Ki cheat me!"

He reported Ma Ki to the sheriff. The sheriff arrested Ma Ki and threw him into jail. Then the landlord went to Ma Ki and shouted, "You fiend, give me back my three hundred pieces of silver or I will have your head!"

"I have spent it," said Ma Ki, who had already shared the money with his friends.

The sheriff said to the landlord, "We shall do anything you want with him."

"Beat him to a pulp!" ordered the angry landlord.

"It will not be hard to do that, Honorable Sir," said the sheriff, "but we shall not be able to bury him today since the ground is frozen. May we beat him tomorrow?"

The landlord replied, "All right, but let him

suffer tonight. Strip him and tie him to the millstone."

The sheriff's men stripped Ma Ki down to his undershirt and tied him to the millstone. As soon as they left him, Ma Ki began to drag the heavy millstone around and around. This activity not only kept him from freezing but actually made him sweat.

In the morning, the landlord sent his servant out to see if Ma Ki had frozen to death. The man returned, saying, "It is very strange, but Ma Ki is perspiring all over!"

The landlord went out to see for himself. He asked, "Do you have a fever, Ma Ki? Why are you sweating in this bitter cold weather?"

"Strange things happen when you wrong a righteous man," replied Ma Ki nonchalantly. "That fox I sold you was really remarkable. Someone must have said something in his presence to offend him. Did your wife say she did not believe in the fox's ability to bring back chickens?"

"Why yes, that's right, but what makes you perspire in this cold?"

Ma Ki said patiently, "Some people can't see a good thing before their eyes. This under-shirt I have on looks like an ordinary enough garment, but it really has unusual qualities. My grandfather left it to me. In freezing weather it keeps me so warm I perspire and in warm weather it keeps me as cool as a cucumber."

The naive landlord believed Ma Ki. He asked, "Will you sell me that undershirt for a hundred pieces of silver?"

"No," said Ma Ki. "Just look what hap-pened the last time I sold you something pre-cious."

"I'll pay you two hundred pieces of silver," said the landlord quickly.

"Well, since I could never refuse you any-thing," relented Ma Ki, "I shall let it go for four hundred pieces of silver."

The landlord returned Ma Ki's clothes to him, set him free, and paid him the money, then went away with Ma Ki's undershirt. Ma Ki ran off with the money to share among his poor neighbors.

The landlord had his servant boil the undershirt in perfumed soap. When it was dried and pressed he took off his brocaded garment, put on the undershirt, and paraded off to visit his friends. Everyone laughed behind his back as he passed. As he became colder and colder, he realized he had been duped again. His wife ran after him and dragged him home before he caught a fatal cold. This was too much for him to bear. The landlord decided he would kill Ma Ki without delay.

The sheriff and his deputy caught Ma Ki, put him in a gunny sack, and strung him up on a thick branch overhanging the sea.

The landlord and the sheriff left the deputy to cut down the branch so that Ma Ki would fall into the water and drown. The deputy started to lift the heavy axe and then noticed it was lunch time. He decided to go home to eat first so as to have enough strength to accomplish his task.

When the deputy had left, the landlord's hunchbacked father-in-law came over the hill to visit his daughter. He was surprised to see a sack tied to a branch overhanging the sea.

Something was struggling inside. "What's up there?" he called.

Recognizing the old man's voice, Ma Ki replied, "It is I. I have been having a hunchback cure and now I am well. My people are supposed to come and cut me down soon. They'd better hurry up for it costs one hundred pieces of silver for every hour I use this sack."

"Imagine that! I happen to be a hunchback, too. If I give you a hundred pieces of silver, will you let me use the sack?"

"All right, but let me down right away before I change my mind!"

"See how straight my back is," said Ma Ki, taking the money from the old man. Then he helped the latter into the sack and strung the sack up to its former position.

After lunch the deputy returned. By this time the landlord had come back to watch. "Hurry up and cut that branch down," ordered the landlord. "He can't escape death this time."

When the hunchback heard what his son-in-law said, he became alarmed and cried, "Let me out. I am your father-in-law!"

"I'll father-in-law you!" screeched the angry landlord, grabbing a spare axe and helping the deputy chop down the branch. The branch cracked and with a loud splash, the sack fell into the sea. The ripples smoothed over the surface, and nothing more was seen of the sack or its contents.

A week later, Ma Ki bought a flock of white geese with the money he had received from the hunchback. The landlord saw him driving the flock.

"Are you a ghost?" asked the astonished landlord.

"No, the pure in heart don't die. When I fell into the sea last week, the Sea King sent his fish soldiers to untie the sack and escort me to his palace. All the furniture was made of gold! They fed me delicacies I have never heard of on land. Beautiful mermaids took me all over the sea, and I was given glittering garments to wear. But I got tired of having nothing to do. The Sea King asked me to choose a wife among the mermaids. I chose the prettiest one but when I wanted to come home to land, she would not accompany me. As a parting gift, the Sea King asked me to choose whatever I wanted from his bulging treasury. When I refused, he asked me why, so I told him how I had two precious things I sold to the landlord and how they brought me all my troubles. Finally, he made me take this flock of geese and made me promise to return often to visit him. All I have to do is to knock eleven times and shout, 'I am Ma Ki, a good and righteous man,' and the palace doors of the Sea will be opened for me."

The landlord was green with envy. He thought what a stupid fool Ma Ki was. If he were so lucky, he would have a harem of mermaids, take everything the Sea King offered, and live a luxurious life.

"Ma Ki," he cooed, "will you take me to the Sea palace if I give you all the wealth I have?"

"Why would I want anything from you when I refused all the riches the Sea King offered me?" asked Ma Ki with indignation.

"Forgive my stupidity, Ma Ki, but please

. 23 .

take me there and I will do whatever you say," begged the landlord.

"Why is it that I can never deny you anything?" asked Ma Ki. "All right, don't tell anyone where you are going. Provide me with a wooden barrel and an iron bar with which to knock, and get yourself an earthenware vat."

The landlord got these things together and they floated out to sea.

"Ma Ki, is it time to start knocking?" asked the impatient landlord.

Ma Ki tapped lightly on his wooden barrel.

The landlord said, "Nobody would hear you. Here, knock loudly on the earthenware vat while I shout, 'I am Ma Ki, a good and righteous man!'"

Ma Ki struck the vat with all his might. The earthenware vessel shattered and the landlord spun to the bottom of the sea.

Stories About a Chinese Simple Simon

The Price of a Pullet

Once a porter decided to treat himself to a pullet for dinner. When he called for the check at the end of the meal, he was told that it would be all right for him to pay later. He thanked the restaurant owner and thought what a kind person he was.

A week later, the porter went to pay his bill. The restaurant owner kept him waiting a long time, adding up the amount he owed. When the check was given to him, the total was several times the market price of a pullet.

In astonishment the porter asked, "How can one chicken cost that much?"

"Very simple!" snapped the restaurant owner. "If you had not eaten that pullet, it would have grown into a hen that laid eggs. The eggs in turn would have hatched into chickens that eventually would become laying hens. This could go on and cost you even more than the amount I put down. So this is the price. I won't accept a copper less."

"You swindler! I won't pay you!" declared the porter.

"All right, let us bring the case before a judge," said the restaurant owner. He dragged the porter to his next-door neighbor, the judge.

Without hesitation, the restaurant owner stated his grievance. The judge decided in his favor, and ordered the porter to pay the amount demanded by the restaurant owner. The porter realized he would not gain anything by further arguments. He asked for a few days to raise the money. This favor was granted by the judge.

Very dejected, the porter left the court. On the road he met a man on a donkey singing a ballad. The porter could see by their similar uniforms that they were members of the same union, but he was so downcast that he merely nodded. The man turned his donkey around and asked what was the matter and if there was anything he could do.

"Who are you?" asked the porter.

"I am Simple Simon," the latter replied.

At this, the porter brightened. Everyone had heard of Simple Simon, the simple, sincere, and straightforward man who was most successful in speaking up for the poor and helpless. The porter told his story from beginning to end.

"Go straight back to the courthouse and say that you want a public trial. I shall defend you," promised Simple Simon.

When the porter demanded a public trial, there was nothing the judge could do but consent. It was the custom in that part of the country to hold public trials for anyone who asked, providing that person was willing to accept double penalty if he lost the case.

On the appointed day of the trial, a crowd collected. Once again the restaurant owner was given an opportunity to tell his story. The restaurant owner took great pains to state the rightness of his case. When it came time for the porter to speak, he said that he was waiting for his lawyer, Simple Simon. This information worried the judge and the restaurant owner, but pleased the crowd, which was looking forward to an interesting trial.

After a while Simple Simon appeared. "I beg the Court's pardon for being late, Your Honor," said Simple Simon, "but I had an important matter to attend to first."

The judge asked, "Can any business be more urgent than the one right here?"

"Well, yes," admitted Simple Simon. "I have to sow wheat tomorrow but the seeds were not roasted and I had to roast three bushels before I could leave."

"What nonsense!" shouted the restaurant owner and judge together. "How can roasted wheat seeds grow?"

Simple Simon answered, "You are absolutely right. Roasted seeds cannot grow. By the same token, how can a chicken lay eggs after it has been eaten?"

"He is right!" shouted all the people. "No

chicken can lay eggs after it has been eaten!"

With public opinion solidly on the side of the porter, the judge had to reverse his earlier decision and allow the porter to pay the fair price for the pullet he had eaten at the restaurant. Thus ended an unfair trial.

Advices

Simple Simon went to the marketplace with hopes of earning some money as a porter. Presently a man approached the group of porters, saying, "I have a crate of china cups and saucers that needs to be transported. The porter who carries it to my home shall receive three pieces of good advice for pay."

None of the porters paid any attention to his offer, but Simple Simon agreed because he thought that money is much easier to come by than good advice.

After they had gone a distance, Simple Simon said, "Let me hear one bit of advice from you."

The man replied, "Beware of the liar who

tells you that it is better to be hungry than to satisfy your stomach."

"That is sensible advice," agreed Simple Simon.

A little later, Simple Simon said, "What is your second piece of advice?"

"Don't let any rogue tell you that it is better to walk than ride," said the man.

Simple Simon, who was quite tired by now, replied, "What fine advice!"

As they came within sight of the man's house, Simple Simon said, "And what is the last piece of advice?"

"Don't believe anyone who tells you there could be a porter more stupid than you!"

As this was said, Simple Simon let the crate crash to the ground. He turned to the man and replied, "And don't believe anyone who tells you that the china in the crate isn't broken!"

The Pot

Simple Simon borrowed a large pot from his wealthy and tight-fisted neighbor.

Several days later Simple Simon went to see this neighbor, saying, "Many, many congratulations to you!"

"For what?" asked the neighbor.

"Your large pot has given birth to a son," answered Simple Simon.

"Nonsense!" said the neighbor. "How is it possible for a pot to have a son?"

"If you don't believe me, see what I have here," said Simple Simon, untying a package enclosing a little pot.

The neighbor thought, "What a fool he is, but if I can benefit from the situation, why not go along with this nonsense." So he replied, "Ah yes, of course I see the resemblance. What a pretty baby. Thank you for bringing it to me. Congratulate the mother, and take good care of her, so that she may bear more children like this one."

A week later, Simple Simon went to the rich neighbor and offered his condolences on the death of the neighbor's big pot.

"Ridiculous!" screamed the neighbor. "How can my pot die?"

Simple Simon retorted, "If a pot can bear a son why can't it die?"

Then the wealthy neighbor realized that it was he who was fooled. He made one last attempt to retrieve his pot by saying, "Very well, since my pot is dead, would you kindly send the corpse to me?"

"I have already buried it at the blacksmith's forge," answered Simple Simon.

"How dare you rob me of my pot, you swindler!" hissed the angry neighbor.

"You robbed me of my little pot first," shouted Simple Simon.

This could have been the beginning of a bitter quarrel, but the wealthy neighbor feared that it would cause him to lose face among the villagers, so he dropped the argument before this subject became common gossip. As it was, Simple Simon made so much noise, the neighbors heard all about the rich man's meanness anyway.

The Shady Tree

In old Cathay there lived a wealthy man in a stately house. A huge cypress tree grew outside this house by the roadside. After dinner the wealthy man would go out and sit under the shade of the tree to enjoy an occasional breeze.

One day a weary peddler plopped himself down in the shade to rest from the broiling sun. The wealthy man came out of his house and ordered the peddler to be gone.

"But what wrong have I committed?" asked the peddler. "The road is public property maintained for the use of all taxpayers."

"Yes, but you are using the shade from the tree I planted and tended for many, many years. I am the only one who has a right to enjoy its shade."

"Very well, will you sell me the shade then?" asked the peddler.

The wealthy man was delighted with the idea of selling the shade from his tree, so he replied, "Why not?"

After they settled on a price, the peddler

insisted on a deed to the sale of the shade before he handed over the amount agreed upon.

Thereafter, he and his friends came to use the shade every day. Sometimes the tree cast its shadow into the courtyard, at other times into the kitchen, and at still other times into the master bedroom. Wherever the shadow fell, the peddler and his friends followed it.

This annoyed the wealthy man beyond endurance. He shouted angrily, "How dare you and your cronies trespass on my property?"

The peddler whipped out the deed from his breast pocket and replied, "Since I own the shade, I shall go wherever it goes."

The wealthy man brought the matter before the court, but nobody was able to help him since the deed proved he had sold the shade, and of course the present owner had exclusive rights to his property. To rid himself of the peddler, who was becoming a great nuisance, the wealthy man asked to buy back the shade, but the peddler refused to sell.

Then one day the wealthy man gave a big party. After all his distinguished guests had arrived in their elegant finery, the peddler strolled in with his ragged friends. They flopped down in the shadow cast by the tree right in the center of the living room. At first the guests were bewildered by this strange sight, but when they learned that the wealthy man had sold the shade they could not stop laughing.

To be made the laughing stock of the town was too much for the wealthy man to bear, so he moved to another province.

The peddler continued to enjoy the shade he had bought. From that day on, all were welcome to stop and enjoy the shade of the cypress tree.

The Three Gifts

There was once a widow who had two sons. The older one had a good head for business, whereas Didi, the younger one, was a simple lad who had no talent for making money, but had a heart of gold. Unfortunately, neither his mother nor brother appreciated this rare human quality. They considered kindness a weakness they were glad to do without. It irked them to see Didi's kind deeds go unrewarded. One day they were especially irritated because they had to go hungry. Didi had given their supper away to a starving family.

"What a fool Didi is!" exclaimed Elder Brother. "Why do we have to put up with such stupidity, Mother?"

"You're right, Son. We must send him out so that he will learn to fend for himself."

The next morning, Didi's mother gave him a dozen rice dumplings and told him not to return until he had made his fortune.

Didi packed his dumplings into his knapsack and set out to make his fortune in the big, wide world.

After hiking all morning, Didi sat down along the seashore and took out a dumpling for lunch. His eyes fell upon a slender snake, a foot long, lying motionless among the pebbles. It lay so still that it looked ill. This moved Didi with pity. He took a long, narrow box from his knapsack and placed the snake gently inside.

Each mealtime he shared his dumplings with

the snake until it outgrew the box. Then he put the snake into a pool, until even the pool became too small for the snake. Finally the snake pleaded, "Please take me to a river or my growth will be stunted."

Didi replied sadly, "All the dumplings are gone. I cannot look after you any longer. My mother said I must try to find my fortune if I wish to go home again."

"Just take me to a river and I will repay you for all your kindness," promised the snake.

Good-natured Didi carried the snake to a big river. As he slipped the snake into the water, the snake turned into a gorgeous dragon with shimmering scales and flowing fins. It said, "Didi, you have been very generous and kind. Before you stands a magic donkey. Whenever you need money, you have only to say to it, 'Give me gold.' However, you must not reveal this secret to anyone."

With these words, the dragon dipped below the water. Didi gazed with an open mouth at the donkey beside him.

"Give me gold," he said. Lo, there was gold.

Didi put the gold pieces into his pocket, got astride the donkey and headed for home. They traveled a long time until finally it became too dark to see. Fortunately, a roadside inn was within view.

Didi dismounted and paid for his room in advance. As the innkeeper led Didi's donkey away, he instructed the man to feed it well, but not to ask the donkey for gold.

The innkeeper agreed. But when everyone was asleep, he returned to the stable and demanded of the donkey, "Give me gold!"

As soon as he had spoken the words, a heap of gold lay at his feet. The innkeeper jumped for joy. He found a donkey that resembled Didi's and substituted it for Didi's magic one.

At the crack of dawn, Didi arose and resumed his homeward journey astride the substitute donkey.

When he arrived home, his mother wanted to know if he had made any money.

"Fetch a rug. This magic donkey will give us as much money as we want."

His mother brought him the rug as Elder

Brother looked on with a sneer.

Didi dragged the donkey onto the rug and demanded, "Give me gold!"

Though he shouted this request repeatedly into the donkey's ear, no gold appeared. Elder Brother doubled over with laughter. His mother was so disgusted that she drove Didi and his donkey away.

Didi returned to the river and cried out, "Oh deceitful dragon, take back your dumb donkey. It will not give gold."

A fountain spouted forth and the dragon surfaced. It made no attempt at explanations, but simply said, "If you don't want the donkey, I shall toss this tablecloth to you. When you are hungry, merely spread it out and ask for whatever food you desire."

Didi walked homeward with the tablecloth. Once more he came to the inn, and again decided to stay there overnight. Before he went up to his room, he left his tablecloth with the innkeeper for safekeeping, with the caution that no one must open the tablecloth and ask for food.

As soon as Didi left, the innkeeper spread out the tablecloth and asked for all the delicacies he could think of. They appeared on the tablecloth that minute. The innkeeper substituted his own tablecloth for Didi's.

Didi woke up early and left with what he thought was his tablecloth. He received scornful looks from Elder Brother as he entered the house. His mother asked him if he had brought her anything. Didi spread out the tablecloth and bid his mother to order whatever she wanted to eat.

His mother said she wanted only a small bowl of rice. Nothing appeared on the tablecloth. No amount of shouting or cajoling produced the least result. Didi's mother was so angry that she pushed him out of the house.

Once more Didi went to the river and called out, "Oh, most ungrateful dragon, why do you tease me? Twice I believed in you, and twice I have been humilated."

The dragon murmured, "I have one more gift for you, this stick of wood. When you stop at the roadside inn tonight, caution the innkeeper not to say, 'Wooden stick, beat me, beat me!' "

Didi did not see any value in the wooden stick, but he was too dejected to argue, so he accepted the stick and trudged home. When he reached the inn, he left the wooden stick with the innkeeper. On the way up to his room, he turned and said, "Oh yes, don't say, 'Wooden stick, beat me, beat me!' "

As soon as Didi had closed the door to his room, the greedy innkeeper, thinking the instructions were a trick of Didi's to deprive him of another treasure, said to the stick, "Wooden stick, beat me, beat me!"

When these words were uttered, the wooden stick rained blows upon the innkeeper without ceasing. He ran to hide, but the stick followed him and struck him on every part of his body. The innkeeper found no respite from the painful whacks of the merciless stick. In desperation, the innkeeper ran to Didi's room and cried, "Please, stop this endless punishment. I'll return your donkey and tablecloth immediately."

Next morning, Didi rode home on his donkey with his tablecloth. With these gifts, his fortune was made forever.

More Fables from the Far East

The Artist

There was once a king who loved the graceful curves of the rooster. He asked the court artist to paint a picture of a rooster for him. For one year he waited and still this order was not fulfilled. In a rage, he stomped into the studio and demanded to see the artist.

Quickly the artist brought out paper, paint, and brush. In five minutes a perfect picture of a rooster emerged from his skillful brush. The king turned purple with anger, saying, "If you can paint a perfect picture of a rooster in five minutes, why did you keep me waiting for over a year?"

"Come with me," begged the artist. He led the king to his storage room. Paper was piled from the floor to the ceiling. On every sheet was a painting of a rooster.

"Your Majesty," explained the artist, "it took me more than one year to learn how to paint a perfect rooster in five minutes."

鳥意 *Life is short, art is long.*

The Trap

A giant clam came up on the sandy shore to enjoy the noonday sun. From the sky, a crane spied the clam and flew down to enjoy a hearty meal. As soon as the crane inserted his beak in the shell's slit, the clam clapped his shell shut on the crane's beak, locking the latter with an iron grip.

. 46 .

Presently the clam said, "If you are not able to fly away in a day or two, you will die of starvation."

To which the crane replied, "If it doesn't rain within a day or two, you will die of thirst."

While they were arguing, a fisherman came by and took the two prisoners away.

🀄 *In the face of mutual destruction, it is fatal to waste time in a debate.*

Heaven and Hell

A Chinese angel visited hell. He saw many people seated around a table covered with delicious food of every description. Beside each person was a pair of yard-long chopsticks. But everyone there was wasting away with starvation, because no one was able to manipulate the clumsy chopsticks adequately to feed himself.

Then the angel went to visit heaven. There he saw another table piled with all kinds of wholesome, delicious food. Each person seated around the table was also provided with yard-

long chopsticks. These people were happy and contented. They were feeding each other across the table with their yard-long chopsticks.

🀫 *The difference between heaven and hell is the people.*

The Turtle and the Herons

Once, on a sparkling lake, there dwelled a turtle and twin cranes. They played together so happily every day that they swore eternal friendship among the three of them. All went well until the year of the dreadful drought. Day after day, week after week, and month after month not a drop of rain fell. Lush gardens turned brown, the thirsty earth became parched, and rivers disappeared. The lake grew smaller and smaller, until the cranes felt they had to fly off to seek a new home. In the evening, they bid farewell to their good friend, the turtle.

"Dear friend, we must go immediately to Heavenly Lake, if we wish to live another day," they told him.

· 49 ·

In tears, the turtle said, "Go ahead and fly to Heavenly Lake by yourselves. When you return next year, you will find my empty shell. I shall be going to another heaven, where friends stick together through thick or thin."

"Boo hoo, hoo," cried one of the cranes. "What else is there to do? We shall all die if we wait till the lake is dry."

Then the other crane spoke. "Maybe we can take you with us. But for my plan to succeed, you would have to do exactly as we say."

"What?" begged the turtle.

"We need to find a suitable stick. You bite the center of it while each of us holds an end in our bill. Under no circumstances during the flight must you open your mouth."

"No problem," boasted the turtle. "Let us start at once."

As soon as they found the right stick, the twin cranes lifted their friend off the ground. In an instant, the three friends were flying over hill and dale.

As they passed over a large field, a farmer said to his co-workers, "Look! Only a brilliant turtle can get two stupid cranes to carry him in such high style."

The cranes paid no attention to such prattle, but the turtle became puffed up with undeserved praise. He began to believe he must be pretty clever to induce his two sincere but simple friends to do his bidding.

On and on they flew. A group of children gathering tea leaves on the hillside looked up and shouted, "Oh, what a smart pair of cranes to think of carrying a creeping creature in the air with them!"

As before, the cranes ignored the remark, but the turtle turned terribly angry.

"They must be made to believe it was my idea," thought the turtle. When he opened his mouth to shout, "Fools!" he fell to his death.

🈂 *False pride goeth before a fall.*

The Fate of Six

Once a flowerpot, a mud cake, a cabbage, a flea, a feather, and a needle came together to talk about the necessary chores of the farm on which they all lived. They immediately elected the flowerpot to be their leader. The flowerpot decided to divide the duties among them thus: The mud cake was to carry water back to the house, the cabbage was to look after the cow, the flea was to tend the ox, the feather was to thresh the grain, and the needle was to sweep the floor.

After issuing these orders, the flowerpot sat back on a shelf like all bosses and waited for the others to report back that the jobs were done.

The mud cake eagerly went out to draw water. In his enthusiasm he spilled water on himself. This carelessness was the cause of his disintegration. Since he was no longer a mud cake, it was no longer possible for him to fetch water.

The cabbage looked after the cow with loving care. He never left the cow's side. Unfortunately the cow did not realize she was being cared for. When she became hungry she naturally looked for the most delicious morsel

nearby, and in one big mouthful the cow ate up the cabbage.

As for the flea, he too tried to do his duty by steering the ox on the right course. The buzzing annoyed the ox so much that he swatted the flea dead with his tail. Of course, with no one to lead them neither the cow nor the ox reached home.

The feather went out to thresh the grain. As soon as he reached the field, a tornado struck and blew the feather into another province. So the feather never returned home.

The needle went out to the barn to make a broom in order to sweep the floor. It got lost in the haystack and never returned home.

The flowerpot sat on the shelf and waited and waited for his staff to report. He became so worried that he jumped off the shelf to see what had happened. And so he was smashed to pieces, for he had forgotten he was only baked clay. Now there isn't even a boss to sit around and give orders.

🈺 *Look before you leap.*

A Gentleman and His Cook

A gentleman had a wonderful cook who knew how to prepare all the dishes he loved. No one else possessed such extraordinary skills in the kitchen. All was well with this gentleman until the cook became tired of her job.

When she gave him her notice to leave, the gentleman offered her more money, better working conditions, and longer vacations. None of those things interested her. Finally, he proposed marriage in order to keep her, and she accepted.

After the honeymoon she told him that he must hire a cook immediately, since a lady in her position could not be expected to do the cooking in the family. When he heard this announcement, the gentleman was so disappointed that he jumped into the river and drowned himself.

🀄 *You cannot eat your cake and still have it.*

The Orange Tree King

Tome was a pauper. His sole possession was an orange tree. This tree became his only reason for existence. He spent his days tending it with the loving care other people lavished on their children or pets. When the oranges were ripe, he guarded the fruits with the jealousy of a lover. Should a boy so much as climb over the fence to reach for one of the golden fruits, Tome would rap the boy's knuckles before he looked at him. He would be lucky to get off with a stern sermon on the sins of stealing, instead of a beating. In time this disciplinarian became known as His Majesty, King Tome of the orange tree.

Early one spring day when the oranges were ripe once more, Tome sat beneath the tree guarding his precious fruits. As night came, his head began to droop and he fell into a slumber. When he woke up he noticed that some of the oranges were missing. The next night, he stood guard again, but try as he would, he was unable to keep from falling

asleep again. This time, many oranges were stolen.

Tome felt he had to find the thief, so he took a nap during the next afternoon and pretended to fall asleep again that night. Between slit eyelids, he saw a fox leap over the fence and make for the oranges without a sound. This angered Tome so much that he grabbed the fox by the end of the tail. He was about to give it a sound thrashing when the animal whipped itself into a ball and flicked away like a lasso. Tome was left standing there with only a fistful of fur to prove that what had happened was not a mere figment of his imagination.

When a neighbor came by, he found a very dejected Tome.

"Tome, why don't you mix a thick pot of paste and pour the mess around the foot of the tree? When the fox comes again, he will stick fast to the ground and you can punish him as you wish," advised the wise old neighbor.

Tome followed that advice and trapped the fox that very same evening. With his club, he was just about to swing a fatal blow at the fox's head when the latter pleaded, "Stop, Your Majesty! Spare my life and I shall serve you the rest of my days. Yes, even to the extent of finding you a loving wife."

"Mock me, will you!" growled Tome, gathering up more strength to smash the fox.

"Don't kill me, not until you have first heard what I can do for you," cajoled the fox. "I know where I can find a princess who will marry you. Her father will be a real king, too."

As unlikely as these wild promises were, they coincided so much with Tome's daydreams that, against his better judgment, he set the fox free.

This surprised even the fox. He decided not to betray the simple trust Tome had placed in him. Immediately the fox went to the king of a far-off kingdom and begged, "May I borrow your sieve? The King, my master, needs one with which to wash his jewels."

Because the king wanted to oblige another king, he lent the sieve to the fox without hesitation. Within the next few days, the fox went to a jeweler and stole a few pearls and pieces of jade, which he pressed between the holes of the borrowed sieve. Then he went to return the sieve. While he was thanking the king, he carelessly dropped the sieve so the pearls and jade rolled out onto the floor.

As the king's three daughters rushed to retrieve them, the fox said casually, "Do such ornaments really please princesses? If I had known earlier, I would have brought you a whole scoop. My master, King Tome, has trunks of them!"

The king was duly impressed. During a reception for the fox, the king let it be known that his eldest daughter was of marriageable age and that he would not be at all adverse to a proposal from young King Tome, if the fox would be kind enough to act as go-between.

The fox said, "Wait! I have no idea whether King Tome is interested in marriage at this time. If I can persuade him to wed your eldest daughter, I shall return and report to you without delay."

When the fox returned, he told Tome that the king had consented to a royal marriage between Tome and the eldest princess. This news was beyond Tome's wildest dreams, and he was overcome with joy. It was not until he turned the matter over in his mind that he saw the absurdity of a match between a pauper and a princess.

However, the fox kept assuring him that he had nothing to fear if he would follow orders. The first thing he advised Tome to do was to wade out to the river surrounding the king's castle and stand in the water up to his head and wait.

Meanwhile the fox hastened to the king and said breathlessly, "My master, King Tome, came with fifty camels bearing gifts for you and his future bride. The crossing was a most unfortunate one. All the camels went under in those swift currents. King Tome would also have drowned if I had not rescued him. Even his clothes were swept away."

The king was overcome with compassion for his future son-in-law who had almost lost his life. He said, "The only important thing is that King Tome lives. Let us make haste to greet him." Turning to a servant, he ordered fine clothes and a horse brought to Tome.

The entire kingdom turned out to welcome King Tome as he rode into the city with his princely garb and grand horse. Soon thereafter, the king threw a ball that lasted three weeks to celebrate the marriage of the eldest princess to Tome.

During the celebration, Tome sought out the fox and expressed his fears of the near future. Again the fox reassured him that all would end well if Tome would but follow orders.

At the end of the wedding celebration, the king gave the couple his royal blessing and ordered an aide and a retinue of soldiers to escort the young couple home.

Before the procession started on its way, the fox stepped forward and said he would run ahead to lead the way and also to forewarn them of any danger that might befall them.

In a short while, the fox met a caravan of camels. When the headman asked the fox why he was running so swiftly, the fox told him he dared not stop, for a group of wild marauders

were killing and looting as they swept across the plains. In the far-off distance from whence the fox had come, the headman saw a horde of riders heading their way. Being outnumbered, the headman became panicky and begged the fox for advice.

The fox said, "When they arrive and ask who owns the camels, simply tell them King Tome does and they will not dare to harm you."

Before the headman could thank the fox, he was gone. When Tome and the princess arrived with the aide and soldiers, the aide asked who owned the camels. The headman immediately said, "They are the property of King Tome!"

The aide said, "What a fine caravan." And to himself, he said, "King Tome must be rich and powerful. Our princess is lucky indeed to have him for a husband."

Next, the fox encountered a pack of horses. The herdsman tending them wanted to know why the fox was in such a hurry. Without reducing speed, the fox shouted over his shoulder that robbers were coming to take the horses and would cut down anyone who tried to stop them. When the frightened man asked what must be done to avoid disaster, the fox suggested that he had only to tell them that the horses belonged to King Tome and they would leave him alone.

When the bridal procession came by, the princess asked who owned the horses.

"King Tome!" the herdsman replied quickly.

This pleased the princess very much, for she admired fine horses.

Presently the fox met a simple shepherd tending his flock. The fox shouted warning of oncoming bandits. Trembling, the shepherd cried for advice. The fox told him to say that the flock belonged to the great King Tome. Again the procession asked who owned the flock, and again they were told they belonged to King Tome.

By now, everyone was thoroughly convinced of the wealth and might of King Tome. Only Tome himself wondered how the fox was able to accomplish these amazing feats of deception.

But this was not all. The fox continued running till he arrived at the palace of the Underworld King. In a mad frenzy, he flung himself from chamber to chamber. When the Underworld King finally stopped the fox to ask the meaning of this rude intrusion, the fox spat out the fearful news. "King Tome, the terrible tyrant, is on his way with his regiments to kill the Underworld King because of a fancied slight. Even I, his advisor, am in danger of losing my life for warning an enemy."

Even as they talked, far-off specks of riders were heading toward the palace. The Underworld King became fearful for his life. It seemed that many people imagined they had reasons to kill him.

"Quick, crawl into the fireplace! I will cover you with logs," ordered the fox.

As the Underworld King did so, the fox tossed an oil lamp on the logs and closed the fire screen. That was the end of the Underworld King.

With the help of the fox, Tome moved into the palace. For many years thereafter, the fox continued to serve Tome as he had promised. Tome asked the fox why he had continued to be so faithful. The fox replied, "A promise made is a debt unpaid!"

On the fox's deathbed, Tome promised he would never forget the fox and that when the fox died he would put the fox on his head. At the fox's funeral, Tome did just that. Thereafter, fur hats became the symbols for promises kept. Though the reason is now long forgotten, wearing hats of fox fur has never gone out of fashion.

About the Author

ISABELLE C. CHANG first heard many of the stories in this book from her Chinese teacher when she was a child growing up in Boston. Years later, she wrote them down for her own children, filling in with her imagination when memory failed her.

Mrs. Chang is a librarian with a bachelor's degree in library science from Simmons College and a master's degree in education from Clark University. She has worked in several libraries in Connecticut and Massachusetts, and at present is with the Shrewsberry, Mass., Junior High School Library. She is married to Dr. M. C. Chang, a scientist, and has three children. Her other books include *Chinese Cooking Made Easy* and *Chinese Fairy Tales*.

About the Artist

TONY CHEN, a graduate of Pratt Institute, has been on the staff of *Newsweek* Magazine since 1961 as a graphic designer and illustrator in the promotion department. He has illustrated six other books, three of them for children. His paintings and sculptures have been exhibited in two one-man shows in New York City.

Mr. Chen was born and raised in the West Indies, in Kingston, Jamaica. He has a special fondness for drawing horses which goes back to his childhood, when he used to watch race horses pass by his house on the way to the tracks. Mr. Chen now lives in Corona, Queens, New York, with his wife and two sons.